MIA MAYHEM #9

AND THE SUPER FAMILY FIELD DAY

BY **KARA WEST**   ILLUSTRATED BY **LEEZA HERNANDEZ**

LITTLE SIMON

New York   London   Toronto   Sydney   New Delhi

LITTLE SIMON
An imprint of Simon & Schuster Children's Publishing Division
1230 Avenue of the Americas, New York, New York 10020
First Little Simon paperback edition September 2020
Copyright © 2020 by Simon & Schuster, Inc.
Also available in a Little Simon hardcover edition
All rights reserved, including the right of reproduction in whole or in part in any form.
LITTLE SIMON is a registered trademark of Simon & Schuster, Inc., and associated colophon is a trademark of Simon & Schuster, Inc.
For information about special discounts for bulk purchases, please contact Simon & Schuster Special Sales at 1-866-506-1949 or business@simonandschuster.com.
The Simon & Schuster Speakers Bureau can bring authors to your live event.
For more information or to book an event contact the Simon & Schuster Speakers Bureau at 1-866-248-3049 or visit our website at www.simonspeakers.com.
Designed by Laura Roode
Manufactured in the United States of America 0421 MTN
2 4 6 8 10 9 7 5 3
This book has been cataloged with the Library of Congress.
ISBN 978-1-5344-7721-6 (hc)
ISBN 978-1-5344-7720-9 (pbk)
ISBN 978-1-5344-7722-3 (eBook)

CONTENTS

CHAPTER 1   THE LETTER (AGAIN!)   1

CHAPTER 2   EXCITEMENT ALL AROUND   11

CHAPTER 3   THE BIG DAY   25

CHAPTER 4   CAPTURE THE FLAG   37

CHAPTER 5   THE RELAY RACE   55

CHAPTER 6   BALLOON DODGEBALL   67

CHAPTER 7   DO THE HOKEYPOKEY   79

CHAPTER 8   TUG-OF-WAR   93

CHAPTER 9   THE AWARDS CEREMONY   105

CHAPTER 10 DÉJÀ VU ALL OVER AGAIN   115

CHAPTER 1

THE LETTER (AGAIN!)

Ever get that funny déjà vu feeling when you know you've totally seen something or been somewhere before?

Well, I just had it!

I opened my mailbox today and right on top was an envelope covered in stamps. I got goose bumps because it looked exactly like an old letter I got that changed my whole life!

You see, I was regular Mia Macarooney until the day a very similar-looking letter arrived. On that day, I found out that I was actually super! Like for real! *I. Am. A Superhero!*

And long story short, my secret superhero name is Mia Mayhem!

I still have a lot to learn, so I go to a top secret academy every day after regular school called the Program for In Training Superheroes, aka the PITS!

So obviously I thought this letter was for me . . . until I looked down and saw it was for my parents!

"Mom! Dad!" I gasped as I ran inside. I had rushed into the kitchen so fast that I bumped right into my dad, knocking over a box of cereal.

Oops!

I would normally clean up right away, but this was more important.

I handed the letter to my mom, who had cereal all over her hair, and eagerly waited for her to open it.

PLOP!

The letter said:

DEAR SARAH AND MARTI MACAROONEY,

I'M SO PLEASED TO INVITE YOU

TO THE PITS SUPER FAMILY

FIELD DAY! GET READY FOR A

FULL DAY OF HEROIC ADVENTURES WITH

YOUR CHILD AS YOU GO UP AGAINST OTHER

FAMILIES AND YOUR FORMER CLASSMATES!

DATE: SATURDAY

TIME: 12–3 P.M.

LOCATION: THE SUPER QT AT THE PITS

SEE YOU THERE!

Dr. Sue Perb

HEADMISTRESS

I was so surprised that I couldn't move. But not my parents. They were totally ready for this. I smiled big as they jumped up and did a double high five over my head.

My mom and dad had come to the PITS with me before, but that was only to meet Dr. Perb before my first day of school. I've never seen my parents in their superhero element before . . . because at home we lead very ordinary lives.

So I have no idea what to expect. But whatever happens this weekend, one thing's for sure: It's going to be SUPER!

EXCITEMENT ALL AROUND

I couldn't stick around at home because it was time for me to get to the PITS.

I ran all the way there and quick-changed into my supersuit. From the outside the PITS looks like a boring empty warehouse. But really, this building has its *own* secret identity too! Because on the inside, this place is a superhero's dream come true.

After the scanner checked my face, the secret entrance appeared, and I sped through the Compass, and up to the second-floor gym.

I spotted my friends as I walked in. Penn Powers, Allie Oomph, and Ben Ocular (along with Ben's guide dog, Seeker) were already there. Just as I expected, they were in the middle of talking about the letters!

"Your parents got them too?" I asked.

Penn and Ben nodded.

"My parents were so excited they eye-lasered the note by mistake," Allie said. "So it went up in flames!"

"Well, my parents decided that dinner this week would be foods starting with *F* and *D* for 'field day,'" said Ben. "So I'm really hoping for fettuccini and doughnuts."

"That's awesome. Mine have already been working on a team high five," Penn said.

"Yeah, mine too! I don't think my dad even noticed I left the kitchen!" I said with a laugh.

There was an excited buzz in the gym. Around us, all the other kids were talking about the same thing.

And that's when a familiar voice rang out—it was Dr. Perb! She was standing with all our PITS professors! There was Professor Stu Pendous, Professor Wingum, Dr. Dash, Professor Dina Myte, *and* Dr. Magni Tude!

"I have some good news and some bad news. The bad news is that we will not have class today—" Dr. Perb said.

A groan went around the gym. But then she gave us the *good* news. "We can't have class today . . . because your professors and I will be at the Super QT getting ready for tomorrow's field day event!"

The Super QT (aka the Super Quick Track) was where I learned how to control my superspeed with Dr. Dash.

"But before we let you leave, I wanted to cover some of the basics first," Dr. Perb continued. "You and your parents will become the ultimate team, as you go up against your classmates in different field day games that we, your professors, have dreamed up for you."

An excited whisper filled the room, and Dr. Perb waited for everyone to quiet down.

"You'll compete in these challenges, sometimes as a family, sometimes on your own, and sometimes in larger groups," she went on. "In each event you'll earn points for your family. Come prepared for anything—but most of all, be ready to have lots of fun!"

After Dr. Perb was done, the room burst into applause as class was officially dismissed.

My friends and I did a quick group high five and said good-bye.

This field day sounds pretty awesome, huh?

If I've learned anything while training to be a superhero, it's that I know everyone is going to bring their A game . . . so I guess, may the best family win!

WOOF!

THE BIG DAY

The next morning I was having a nice dream about a chocolate cake when someone knocked on my door.

"Mia?" It was Mom, who was up waaaay too early for a Saturday. "What are you still doing in bed?!"

"It's field day!" came Dad's voice. "You can't sleep in now!"

"Oh yeah, wanna bet?" I mumbled.

But in the end I couldn't stay in bed. They kept knocking on my door until I joined them in the backyard. They were doing a bunch of warm-ups, while I kept trying to just keep my eyes open.

Now, don't get me wrong. I'm really excited for today.

But like Dr. Perb said, I thought field day was supposed to be fun!

Not something that was supposed to be taken *this* seriously. But I have to admit, I loved seeing how excited my parents were. Finally, several hours later (after we were very warmed up), we headed over to the PITS.

As soon as we arrived, I quick-changed, like usual. But then, something strange happened.

They both quick-changed too! I'd never seen them in their supersuits before! It was AH-MAZING, let me tell you.

They weren't my mom and dad anymore, they were Sarah Spectacular and Marti Marvelous!

My mouth dropped to the floor as I stood in shock.

I only snapped out of it when my dad told me to follow them inside.

Today the building was bustling with superhero families as we made our way to the back door. I didn't even need to lead the way because my parents knew exactly where to go!

Once we were outside, we were under a giant invisible dome. The protective shield covered the QT track and the whole field next to it—that way, regular people would never see a bunch of superheroes flying around.

Pretty smart, huh?

When we got to the track, I wanted my parents to meet my friends' moms and dads—but get this: They were *already* friends! My dad happily said hello to Penn's dads, while Mom and Allie's mom talked about a mission they had in the Arctic. Can you believe it?

My friends and I looked at each other and shook our heads. Dr. Perb was right. This day *was* going to be full of surprises.

Soon Dr. Perb appeared at the top of a tall podium and waved to the crowd.

"Welcome, students and parents, to the first ever Super Family Field Day at the PITS! We will have lots of awesome events throughout the day," she said, "but today's ultimate goal is simple.

The family with the most points by the end of the day will be awarded this PITS Super Family Field Day trophy!"

Professor Stu Pendous held up the prize, and I watched as it sparkled in the light.

We waited for Dr. Perb to give us the first set of instructions as the headmistress took a deep breath.

"This first game will be for our current students only," she announced. "Get ready for capture the flag!"

CAPTURE THE FLAG

With that, Professor Wingum flew up and grabbed the microphone.

"The goal of the game is to grab the other team's flag and return it to your own side! However, there will be a special twist." He snapped his fingers, and then suddenly the space under the dome was filled with floating rings, hovering hurdles, and moving ropes.

"Obviously, we had to make it a little bit harder for all you talented heroes, so you'll also be flying through this obstacle course!"

Our parents wished us luck, and
then my friends and I quickly made a
team. Ben and Seeker were going to
guard our flag while the rest of us were
going to go up against the other team.

Once everyone was in their positions in the air, the whistle sounded, and the game began!

We cheered as the first kid on our team took off through the starting hoop—where she set off a loud buzzer. Disqualified for touching the side!

So the next kid flew off, but he got tangled up in the moving ropes. Again, disqualified!

Just like that, kids were dropping like flies, and the other team was moving faster!

I knew we had to do something, so the closer I got to my turn, the more nervous I got.

I could tell Penn was too because he kept looking back at me as we inched forward.

Soon a buzzer sounded, and it was his turn. As Penn flew up, Allie and I cheered at the top of our lungs. But less than a minute later, he tripped in midair. Again, he was disqualified.

Next up was Allie, and she moved superfast. As she got past the halfway mark, I thought she might be the first one to make it to the other side . . .

until *BEEP! BEEP! BEEP!*

She set off a
buzzer on a very
tricky hoop.

Just like that, Allie was out too.

I took a deep breath and started the course. Now it was up to me.

Down below, I could hear all the parents cheering, but I didn't dare look—it was going to take all my focus to get through this.

I flew through each hoop, careful to
not touch the edge of the ring, when I
heard a voice.

"Watch out, Mia!" cried Allie, just
in time for me to avoid the swinging
rope that was coming my way. *Whew!*
What a close call!

I ducked and dodged each moving target until believe it or not, I made it to the other side! I'd done it! I looked back and saw all my friends cheering for me. Now all I needed to do was get the other team's flag. But my stomach dropped as soon as I saw who was guarding it.

Oh no.

It was Hugo Fast. The one kid I hoped it wasn't going to be.

I took a deep breath and dashed behind him for the flag. And that's when I heard Penn and Allie yell out, "HEY, LOOK HERE!"

And their distraction worked! Hugo
looked away just long enough for me to
grab the flag and fly back to our side.

My teammates and friends crowded around me and lifted me into the air. WE WON . . . because of me!

Once we got back down on the ground, as expected, Hugo pushed past me in a huff. But nothing was going to put me in a bad mood, because everyone on my team got ten points, while I got twenty!

The race for first place was officially on, and things were looking super!

CHAPTER 5

THE RELAY RACE

When Dr. Dash took the spotlight next, it was clear that the games weren't going to get any easier.

"This is an *egg*-stra special sack relay race!" he announced. "Because you will also be carrying an egg on a spoon, using only your mouth!"

"Wooo-hooo!" my mom cried out. "Let's do this!"

I smiled big as my mom grabbed one of the sacks.

"Are you sure that's the way you want to wear it?" Dad asked, confused as he watched my mom wrap the corner around her wrists.

"Don't worry, honey. I'm a sack-racing expert," Mom said, raising her eyebrows.

"Because what if you—" Dad reached out to adjust the sack, but Mom shot him a look that made him yank his hand back pretty fast. "You know, you're right, honey. That sack technique looks terrific!" he said quickly as he winked at me.

"Thank you, sweetheart," Mom said. "Now let's have some fun!"

Once everybody had lined up at the starting line, Dr. Dash blew his whistle. My parents decided I should go first, so I took a small jump forward, holding the sack as tightly as I could. But this was definitely harder than it looked!

The spoon and egg wobbled with my every move.

Out of the corner of my eye, I could see Hugo a few rows down. He'd tried to go fast, but his egg immediately plopped off and hit the ground.

I shouldn't have looked, though, because then on my next hop, I dropped *my* egg too! So I ran back to the starting line, got a new egg, and hopped a couple times before it happened *again*!

By this point, I wanted to give up. But that's when I heard my parents cheering me on.

"Take all the time you need!" yelled Mom.

"Slow . . . ," Dad cheered.

"And steady!" Mom finished.

They were the best cheerleaders a kid could have. I took a deep breath, and slowly but surely, I finally made it all the way across!

After that, it was my mom's turn. She jumped down the track with the egg carefully balanced on the spoon. And guess what? She did it without breaking a single egg!

Turns out she really was a sack-race expert!

Then it was my dad's turn, and he . . . was not quite as controlled as my mom.

He kept dropping the egg, and every time he did, he made the funniest face.

By the time he finally made it across, my mom and I were rolling on the floor. We were nowhere near first place, but I couldn't stop laughing.

By the last round, Allie's family won first place. And Penn and Ben's families tied for second! We tied too, with none other than Hugo's family.

Judging by Hugo's face, he was *not* happy with these results.

But for me, this day was just getting better and better, and I couldn't wait to see what was next!

CHAPTER
6

BALLOON DODGEBALL

For the next round the professors announced a dodgeball tournament!

This game was going to be family versus family, and the winner of each game would go on to battle another team. Eventually, there would only be two, and the winner of that final knockout round would be the dodgeball champion!

Dodgeball was one of my favorites, so I was ready to get down to business.

For our first round, it was my family against Allie's family.

Professor Stu Pendus was our referee. We listened as he explained the rules.

"If you step outside these lines, you'll hear a buzzer and be out of the game," he explained. "Here are your balloons!"

We each got a huge supply of balloons filled with water, confetti, tomato sauce, slime, glitter—everything you could imagine!

My family and Allie's family shook hands (for good sportsmanship), and then Professor Stu Pendus stepped out of the way.

"Get ready! This is going to be messy," he said with a smile. Then he blew his whistle.

WEEP!

And believe me, messy was right!
I flew into a somersault to avoid a
red balloon while Mom used her heat
lasers to pop one. Meanwhile Allie did
a midair split over a purple balloon.

And her dad used his breath to create a wind tunnel that knocked out three balloons at once!

But my family put up a good fight, so after the most epic battle and many close calls, my parents and I won the round. Allie was such a good sport about it that we hugged and she wished me luck.

I smiled big because we needed all the luck we could get.

By the time it came down to the final two teams, it was my family . . . and Hugo's.

We took our places on either side of the dividing line. And as we waited for the whistle, the knot in my stomach grew bigger and bigger.

TWEET!

All six of us grabbed balloons and let them fly at the same time!

As soon as I ducked below a pink balloon on my left, my mom yelled, "Look out!" and dove to save me from a blue one on my right!

Just like that, we were down a person . . . until I hit Hugo's dad with a giant glitter balloon!

And after that, things went really fast.

Hugo's mom got tagged out, and then so did my dad.

Soon, as the clock counted down the last few seconds, it was just me and Hugo, face-to-face.

I took a deep breath and closed one eye.

This was going to be close.

We lifted our balloons and threw at the exact same time.

Then I moved out of the way as fast as I could.

DO THE HOKEYPOKEY

But it was too late!

SPLAT!

I looked up as tomato sauce dripped down my face.

Hugo got me, and his family won!

I couldn't believe it. I was SO close.

Only to lose it all in the last second!

I turned around slowly and looked at my parents.

Mom was covered in slime. And my dad?

He was covered in confetti.

I wasn't in a great mood, but let me tell you, as soon as we saw one another we all burst out in laughter.

Just as we were doing our best to clean off, I heard a weird quacking noise behind me. Our professors were getting ready for the next game.

I watched as a bunch of animals paraded through the center of the field. There were cats, dogs, ducks, and pigs—and a very cute little baby piglet!

"For this next game," Dr. Tude announced, "families may choose any member of their team. This person will be responsible for leading a group of these animals around the Super QT and then dancing the hokeypokey!"

Ha! Did you hear that?

I knew right away that this would be perfect for one particular person.

"Dad!" I cried. "This game was made *just* for you!"

"Are you sure?" he asked.

"Oh definitely!" my mom and I exclaimed.

My dad was a veterinarian and talking to all kinds of animals was what he did best!

So my dad nodded and walked over to take his place at the starting line. He had two cats, one French poodle, a duck, and the baby pig I'd seen earlier. I could tell he was nervous because he kept glancing over his shoulder and smiling at us. We gave him four giant thumbs-up, and then the whistle blew!

Right away I knew this wasn't going to be easy. The poodle was pretty chill, but the cats were *too* chill. They just wanted to take a nap on the starting line. Meanwhile the duck stood up and started waddling in the other direction. And the baby pig? He was so excited

by the whistle that he just started running!

It was a hilarious disaster! But at least everybody was having the same problem, right?

I watched as my dad calmly tried talking to each of the animals.

A few minutes later something unbelievable happened!

They made a single-file line, and they started making their way around the Super QT!

Hugo's mom was the only other person who had managed to do the same. She was doing well, but Hugo

looked *way* too stressed out that it was making me nervous too!

Dad got to the end of the lap first, and he began telling the animals to stand in a circle to dance the hokeypokey.

Soon, with some music on, I watched in awe as all the animals put their right legs in, then pull them out.

My dad was really teaching them how to dance!

But right then Hugo's mom got into position with her animals and knew exactly what to do. She started singing, and all the animals did all the steps, as if they were trained!

It was so incredible that even my Dad stopped to watch.

So in the end, even though my dad did well, and again, was so close, Hugo's mom ended up winning.

Which unfortunately meant one thing: Everything was going to ride on the last game of the day.

TUG-OF-WAR

When everyone was gathered, Professor Dina Myte grabbed the microphone. "The final event of the day is SUPER tug-of-war! The top two teams will be the team captains—so Mia Mayhem and Hugo Fast, please pick your teammates!"

I picked my team pretty easily, which included Penn, Allie, Ben, and their families.

Then, after Hugo finished, we all lined up.

It turns out that super tug-of-war isn't exactly the same as the tug-of-war you might know.

Because instead of a rope, we were using a really heavy steel pipe!

We all lined up along the huge piece of metal. Since we were team captains, instead of the front, Hugo and I stood at the very ends, behind everyone on our team.

Now, I'm pretty strong, and I've carried some really heavy things before, *including* a gigantic robot. But to be honest, I was sweating bullets. So much was riding on this last game!

And my parents could tell it was bothering me because my mom turned around.

GULP!

"Remember, this is all just for fun, Mia," my mom said.

"Yeah, there's nothing to worry about!" Dad said cheerfully.

I tried to smile, but my hands were clammy, and I could see Hugo at the opposite end, giving me a serious look.

Professor Myte nodded at us to give us a signal.

"Okay. Ready? Set?" She blew the whistle. "Go!"

The tug-of-war was on!

For a moment, the pipe was completely still as both teams pulled equally hard. Then Hugo's team let out a big grunt as they pulled us forward a few feet.

Oh no! We needed to act fast.

"On the count of three, everybody, pull!" I yelled. Slowly but surely I walked my team backward. It was working!

I just needed to get back far enough
to grab the flag on the cone.

But before I knew it we were being
pulled forward again.

I tried to rally my team as much
as I could, but I was getting more and
more tired, and the tug-of-war battle
was getting harder and harder . . . until
finally, Hugo's side made one last big
pull—and they got us over the line.

That was it. After all that, they won.

They started cheering and high-fiving one another, while our team tried to catch our breath.

"Aw, Mia. We tried our best," Allie said with a shrug.

"Yeah, we did because I can't lift my arms!" Ben groaned.

Allie and Penn laughed, but I couldn't break a smile. It didn't seem fair that we lost—we'd tried and were SO close!

And it definitely didn't help to see Hugo jumping around yelling, "I'm number one!"

Yeah, this loss definitely didn't feel good. At. All.

CHAPTER
9

THE AWARDS CEREMONY

Soon, it was awards ceremony time, but I was in no mood to stay. "Can we just go home?" I asked Dad, pulling him.

"And miss the awards?" he asked.

"It's not like we're getting one," I mumbled.

That's when Mom knelt next to me. "But we didn't come to win a trophy, we came to have fun, remember?"

"Really?" I asked. "Is that why you did all that warming up this morning? So you could *not* win?"

Dad put a hand on my shoulder. "We just wanted to have the most fun possible. And we did! Sometimes you try hard, and you don't win—and that's okay."

"And anyway, you always get the number one trophy in our hearts, honey," Mom said, bopping my nose.

I really wasn't in the mood to be mushy. But the more I thought about it, I did feel better because they were right—I *did* have a lot of fun.

So we headed back to the ceremony just in time to see Professor Wingum hand the trophy to a very happy Hugo.

Even though I really wanted the trophy to be ours, I still clapped for him and his team.

Because being a good sport is more important than winning.

After Hugo and his parents finished taking pictures, I thought it was over, but then Dr. Perb kept talking.

"And now there's one extra trophy we'd like to give. We'd like to name a Field Day MVP—the Most Valuable Player! This is someone who worked incredibly hard and was an excellent leader and teammate.

"Today's MVP award goes to: MIA MAYHEM!"

WHAT? Did you just hear that?

I couldn't believe it! I looked at my parents, who were beaming with pride. Up onstage, Dr. Perb gave me a hug, and then I turned to face the crowd.

I grabbed the trophy and gave Dr. Perb a big hug.

"Thank you for this award! But this isn't just mine. It also belongs to everyone on my team. I couldn't have been a good teammate without the best superheroes around!"

Then the audience cheered. And it was in that moment that I knew my parents were right. Having fun with my friends and being the best teammate I could be was better than winning.

CHAPTER 10

DÉJÀ VU ALL OVER AGAIN

After the most fun field day ever, I slept for the rest of the weekend.

That field day was the most amazing and exhausting thing I'd ever done. But, luckily, by Monday, I was feeling back to normal. I met my best friend, Eddie, for the walk to school, and I told him all about it. (He's one of the few people who knows about my secret identity.)

At one point he was so surprised he completely stopped walking. "They actually made you do the hokeypokey with the animals?"

I laughed and nodded. Sometimes I forget how totally bananas my life might seem to non-superheroes!

We got to school and sat at our desks, and then our teacher wrote something in big letters across the whiteboard.

And that's when my jaw dropped.

Remember what I said earlier about that funny déjà vu feeling where you feel like you've seen something or been somewhere before?

Well, do you see what I'm seeing written on that board?

Yeah, that's right. It's FIELD DAY this weekend . . . and I have to bring my parents!

Eddie and I looked at each other and burst into laughter.

I couldn't believe I was going to have to do this all over again in just one week!

Part of me was excited because field day might honestly be my favorite day ever.

But then I realized something.

I've never been part of a regular school field day before. And neither have my parents!

Was it going to be possible for three superheroes to go to a regular school field day without causing total mayhem?

I have no idea.

But I have a weird, funny feeling that this regular, totally non-superhero field day is going to get crazy.

I can only hope that things don't get *too* out of hand.

And one thing's for sure: By the end of it all, may the best family win!